READING CORNER

Jack the Fearless

Written by
Enid Richemont

Illustrated by
Beccy Blake

W
FRANKLIN WATTS
LONDON•SYDNEY

Enid Richemont

"I like dancing, eating avocadoes and making up stories. I'm fond of donkeys, too, but I'd rather have a cat on my lap!"

Beccy Blake

"I like illustrating because I like to draw dragons. The nearest I got to being a dragon was in my school play!"

Jack the Fearless

A humorous story

First published in 2006 by
Franklin Watts
338 Euston Road
London
NW1 3BH

Franklin Watts Australia
Hachette Children's Books
Level 17/207 Kent Street
Sydney
NSW 2000

A CIP catalogue record for this book is available from the British Library.

ISBN 0 7496 6546 7 (hbk)
ISBN 0 7496 6552 1 (pbk)

Series Editor: Jackie Hamley
Series Advisors: Dr Barrie Wade, Dr Hilary Minns
Design: Peter Scoulding

Printed in China

For Billy and Tom, with love – E.R.

Jack was a weaver, but he dreamed of becoming a knight.

One day he painted his knight's
name on a saucepan lid:
Jack the Fearless.

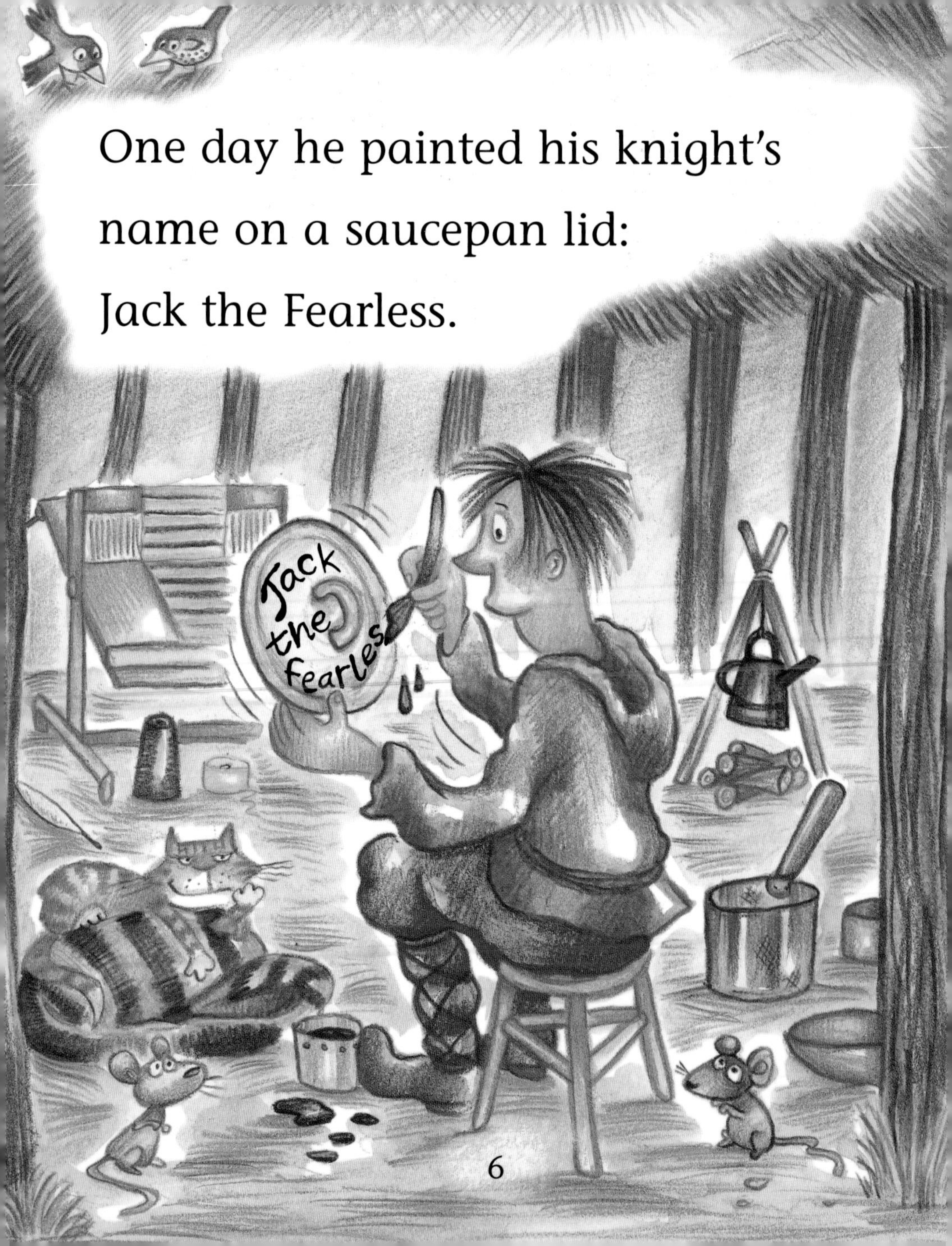

Then he put the saucepan on his head and picked up a stick.

He went to see his old donkey, Alfie, who was busy eating carrots.

"I'm Jack the Fearless now," he cried.

"I've got a helmet, a shield and a sword. All I need is a horse."

"Eee-aaaw," sighed Alfie.

Jack decided to have an adventure. He dragged Alfie away from his carrots.

They plodded along the road
until they came to a castle.

The king was looking out of his window. "Jack the Fearless," he read. "Just the man I need."

The king held a feast for Jack.
"Tomorrow," he declared,
"you will fight the great dragon."

Next morning, the king brought out a splendid new saddle for Alfie.

Jack climbed slowly into the saddle.

He was already feeling scared.

The king whispered into Alfie's ear: "Carrots for ever if you've fought the dragon by tea time."

And suddenly Alfie was off,

galloping like the wind.

After a while, Jack smelt a terrible smell. He saw people running.
"Turn back!" they yelled.
"The great dragon's coming!"

Jack the Fearless

"Stop, Alfie!" Jack cried. He tried pulling on the reins, but Alfie wouldn't stop.

Jack grabbed a tree branch.

"I'll be safe up here," he thought as Alfie galloped away.

Below, the dragon
started sniffing.
"I smell a man!"
she hissed.

Then she yawned. "But I've already eaten twenty children, so I can wait for my pudding."

The dragon closed her eyes and started to snore.

"Now's my chance," thought Jack, and he began to scramble down. CRACK! A branch snapped, and he fell astride the dragon's neck.

The dragon woke up. “My pudding!” she roared. She turned her head to bite him, but Jack grabbed her horns.

Then the dragon rose, blazing, into the air. She wriggled as she flew, trying to shake Jack off.

She was still wriggling when she flew SPLAT! into the castle walls.

Jack was thrown from her neck,

and landed back on to Alfie.

"You've killed the dragon!" cried the king. He was delighted. He gave Jack a castle, and Alfie his very own field of carrots.

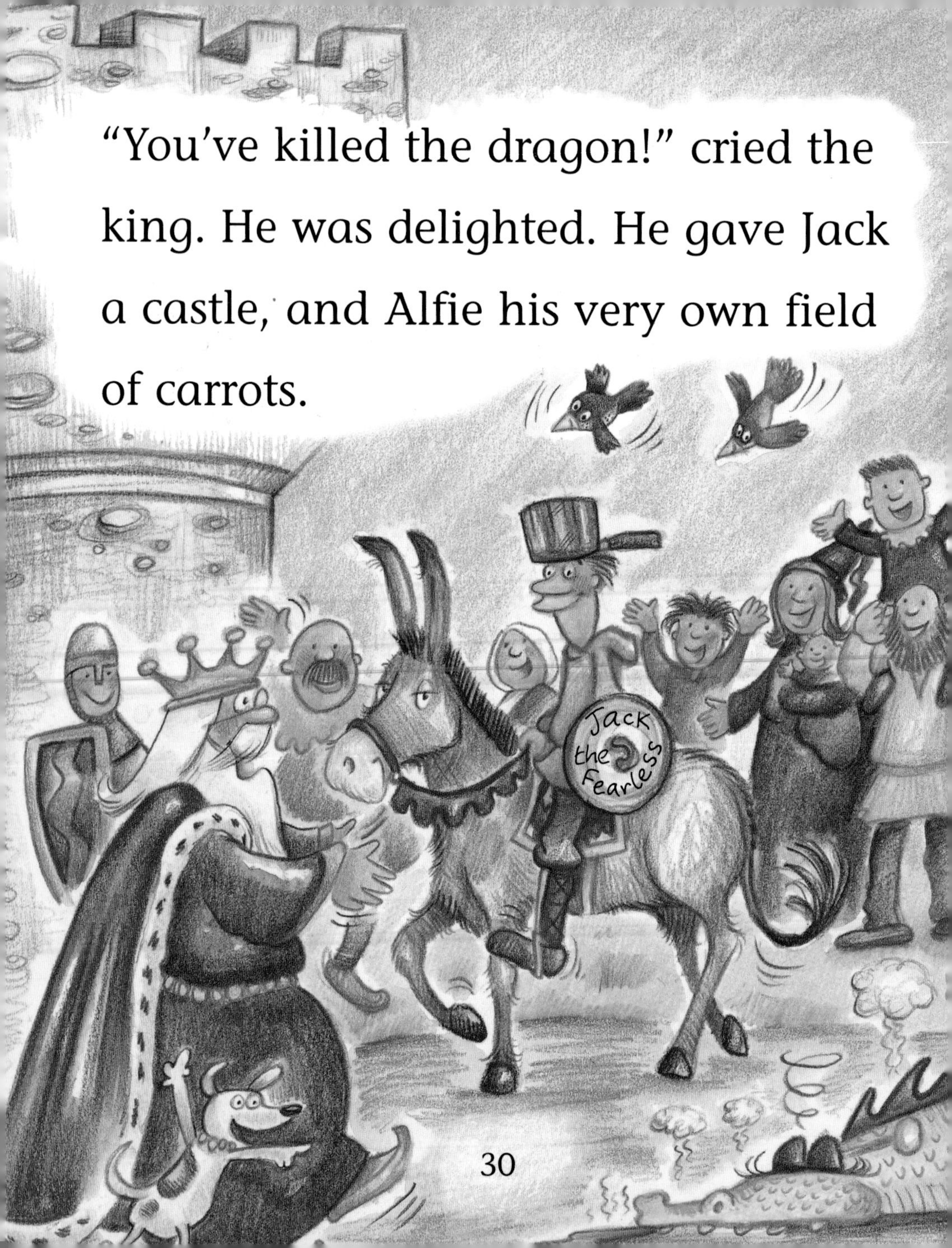

And Sir Jack the Fearless and Lord Alfie Carrot lived happily ever after.

Notes for parents and teachers

READING CORNER has been structured to provide maximum support for new readers. The stories may be used by adults for sharing with young children. Primarily, however, the stories are designed for newly independent readers, whether they are reading these books in bed at night, or in the reading corner at school or in the library.

Starting to read alone can be a daunting prospect. READING CORNER helps by providing visual support and repeating words and phrases, while making reading enjoyable. These books will develop confidence in the new reader, and encourage a love of reading that will last a lifetime!

If you are reading this book with a child, here are a few tips:

1. Make reading fun! Choose a time to read when you and the child are relaxed and have time to share the story.

2. Encourage children to reread the story, and to retell the story in their own words, using the illustrations to remind them what has happened.

3. Give praise! Remember that small mistakes need not always be corrected.

READING CORNER covers three grades of early reading ability, with three levels at each grade. Each level has a certain number of words per story, indicated by the number of bars on the spine of the book, to allow you to choose the right book for a young reader:

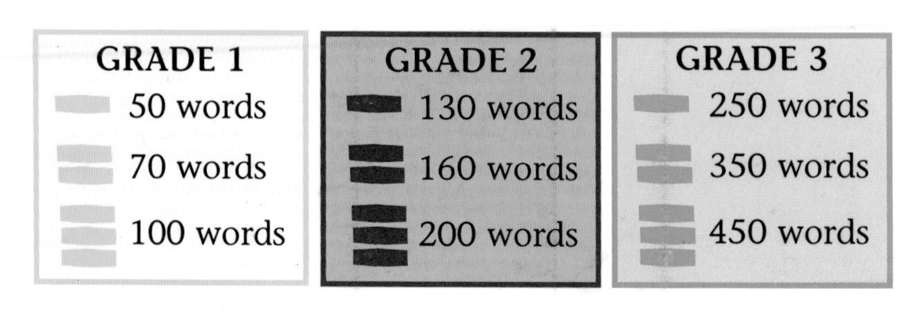

GRADE 1	GRADE 2	GRADE 3
50 words	130 words	250 words
70 words	160 words	350 words
100 words	200 words	450 words